Training Tallulah

ROSIE REEVE

Tom and Tallulah are not exactly
best friends right now . . .

WALKER BOOKS FOR YOUNG READERS
AN IMPRINT OF BLOOMSBURY
NEW YORK LONDON NEW DELHI SYDNEY

When Tom met Tallulah he was **extremely** shy—
too shy to even come out of his box.

He was just a pair of furry ears.

"Hello!"

said Tallulah.

"Meow?"

said the ears.

But Tallulah knew **exactly** what to do to make Tom feel at home.

She put a tiny saucer of milk outside his box and waited... and waited.

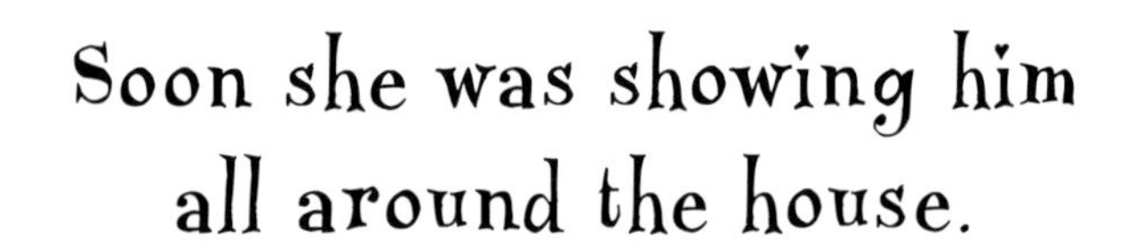

Soon she was showing him all around the house.

She even drew a map so he could find the best places for catnapping.

It was a catnap map.

Tallulah showed Tom his very own door.

She even made him
a special toy.

Tom was amazed at how well Tallulah understood **Cat**.
She seemed to know exactly what he wanted
from a simple **purr** or a **meow**.

Caring for
Your New
Kitten

In no time at all, Tom had settled into his new home perfectly.

Tom decided that since Tallulah seemed to be so good at **Cat**, he should try to learn **Human**.

But he didn't tell anyone.

He just secretly followed Tallulah around
and took notes in his little sketchbook.

One morning, Tom got up
and went to the bathroom.

He brushed his teeth
and combed his whiskers.

Then he got dressed...

and had breakfast.

By the time Tallulah came downstairs,
Tom had already made her
a special toy to play with.

But while Tom seemed to be getting
better and better at **Human**,
Tallulah's **Cat** was not improving **at all**.

She got in a tangle with the string.

She spilled her milk.

She got stuck in the door.

And she catnapped in all the **wrong** places!

But Tom remembered how patient
Tallulah had been with him.

So he waited . . . and waited . . .

Before long, Tallulah began
to settle into things nicely.

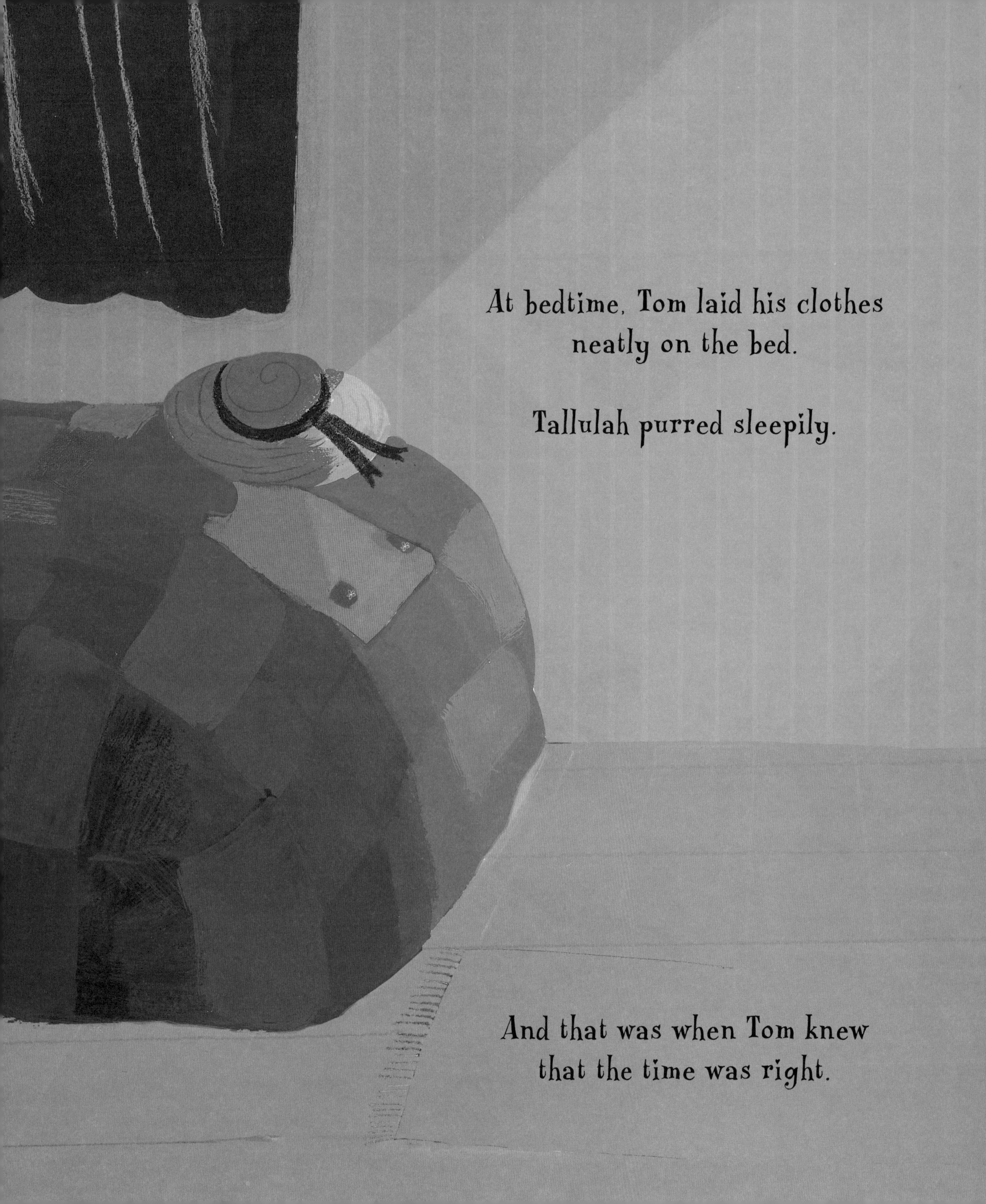

At bedtime, Tom laid his clothes
neatly on the bed.

Tallulah purred sleepily.

And that was when Tom knew
that the time was right.

The next morning, Tom got up early
and went to the pet shop.

"She's totally housebroken," he said.
"She'll make the perfect pet for somebody.

But could I exchange her . . ."

FISHBITES
The purrfect
treat for puss
FLEA-AWAY
No more
scratching!
SQUEAKY WHEEL OIL
Buy one,
get one
free!

". . . for a **puppy**?"

"Hmmm . . . I might have taken this too far . . ."

First published in Great Britain as *When Tom Met Tallulah* in April 2013 by Bloomsbury Publishing Plc
Published in the United States of America in January 2014 by Walker Books for Young Readers, an imprint of Bloomsbury Publishing, Inc.
www.bloomsbury.com

For information about permission to reproduce selections from this book, write to Permissions, Walker BFYR, 1385 Broadway, New York, New York 10018
Bloomsbury books may be purchased for business or promotional use. For information on bulk purchases please contact Macmillan Corporate and Premium Sales Department at specialmarkets@macmillan.com

Library of Congress Cataloging-in-Publication Data
Reeve, Rosie.
Training Tallulah / Rosie Reeve.
pages cm
Summary: Tallulah easily makes her new kitten, Tom, feel at home, but Tom decides that since Tallulah makes such a good cat, he should learn to be human.
ISBN 978-0-8027-3590-4 (hardcover)
[1. Cats—Training—Fiction. 2. Animals—Infancy—Fiction. 3. Humorous stories.] I. Title.
PZ7.R25577Tr 2014 [E]—dc23 2013010712

Art created with mixed media
Typeset in Tom&Tallulah
Book design by Zoe Waring

Printed in China by C&C Offset Printing Co., Ltd., Shenzhen, Guangdong
2 4 6 8 10 9 7 5 3 1

All papers used by Bloomsbury Publishing, Inc., are natural, recyclable products made from wood grown in well-managed forests. The manufacturing processes conform to the environmental regulations of the country of origin.